Bernard F. Moore

The Rough Rider

a play in four acts

Bernard F. Moore

The Rough Rider
a play in four acts

ISBN/EAN: 9783337391461

Printed in Europe, USA, Canada, Australia, Japan

Cover: Foto ©Andreas Hilbeck / pixelio.de

More available books at **www.hansebooks.com**

THE ROUGH RIDER

A PLAY IN FOUR ACTS

By BERNARD FRANCIS MOORE

AUTHOR OF "CAPTAIN JACK," "THE IRISH AGENT," "BROTHER
AGAINST BROTHER," ETC., ETC.

BOSTON

1898

THE ROUGH RIDER.

CHARACTERS.

JAMES CRAWFORD, *a Cuban planter, formerly of New York City.*
ROBERT HAMILTON, *his secretary, afterwards a captain of the " Rough Riders," U. S. V.*
RAMON MARANA, *overseer of the plantation, and a wolf in sheep's clothing.*
DON LOUIS MARANA, *his son, afterwards a Spanish cavalry captain.*
DENNIS RAFFERTY, *a product of the Emerald Isle and a corporal in the " Rough Riders," U. S. V.*
SAM JACKSON, *an American of dark color, and Robert's body servant.*
PEDRO, *a Cuban spy.*
ALMA CRAWFORD, *the planter's daughter.*
INEZ, *her maid, a young Cuban girl.*

AMERICAN AND SPANISH SOLDIERS, ETC.

ACT FIRST.—The Crawford Plantation—Santiago, Cuba—May, 1898—Gathering Clouds.

ACT SECOND.—"With the Boys in Blue."—In the Trenches—July, 1898—Kidnapped.

ACT THIRD.—A Room in the Fort—The Prisoners—The fall of Santiago !

ACT FOURTH—The Crawford Plantation—Six Months Later—After the Struggle—The Stars and Stripes over All.

COSTUMES.

JAMES CRAWFORD. Brown linen coat, pants and vest ; soft shirt and black string tie, straw hat, mixed gray wig, short mixed gray beard.

ROBERT HAMILTON. White linen pants and coat, soft shirt and tie, straw hat, for Acts First and Fourth. Uniform of a Captain of the "Rough Riders," for Acts Second and Third. Sword and pistols for Act Second only. Black curly wig.

RAMON MARANA. White linen coat and pants, soft shirt and tie for Act First. Uniform of an officer of the Spanish army for Act Third Beard and wig of black.

LOUIS MARANA. White linen coat and pants, soft shirt and tie, straw hat for Act First. An old tattered pair of pants, blue flannel shirt, tattered straw hat, one suspender holding pants up, face and hands almost black for Act Second. Uniform of a Spanish captain in Act Third. Same costume, with the addition of a coat and scrubby beard for Act Fourth.

DENNIS RAFFERTY. White overall, calico shirt and straw hat for Act First. Uniform of a corporal of "Rough Riders," for Act Second. Same costume as Act First for Act Fourth. Red wig and mustache.

SAM JACKSON. Blue overalls and calico shirt with sleeves rolled up, overalls, and blue soldier jacket and hat for Act Second. A Spanish coat and cap with gun for Act Third. Same costume as Act First for Act Fourth. Black hands and face, kinky wig.

PEDRO. Old black ragged pants and coat, straw hat for Acts Second and Third. White overalls and calico shirt for Act Fourth. Face and hands darkened.

ALMA CRAWFORD. White muslin dresses trimmed with blue ribbons for Acts First and Fourth. White duck skirt and jacket, pink waist, hat to match, for Acts Second and Third. Blonde wig.

INEZ. Dark red skirt and black waist, black lace scarf wrapped around neck, face and hands of a dark brown color, but not as black as Pedro's.

THE ROUGH RIDER.

ACT I.

SCENE.—*A pretty interior. Large door* C. *opening into a garden. Door* L. *opening into another room. Window* R., *half open, white muslin curtain on window, tied back with blue ribbons ; cane-seated sofa down* L., *desk and chair down* R., *straw matting on the floor. On the wall* L. C. *a medium sized American flag. The room has a cool and inviting look.*

> [JAMES *is seated at desk writing. The sound of a piano is heard from off* L. *playing the " Union Forever," as the curtain rises, gradually growing fainter, until it dies out altogether.*

James (*listening and then with a sigh*). The " Union Forever." What memories does not that old song recall. Will the time ever come when this beautiful down-trodden island will be free from the yoke of the Spanish government ? Will the destruction of the " Maine " in the harbor of Havana, be the means of adding the single star of the insurgents' flag to the glorious old stars and stripes ! Will the time ever come when this fertile island will be under the protection of the American government ?   [*Begins to write again.*

RAMON **enters** *from* L.

Ramon (*removing hat and bowing*). Good-morning, Senor Crawford.

James (*turning around in surprise and then nodding*). Ah, you, Ramon. What is it you wish to say to me ? Has anything happened of importance ? Has news been received from Washington, about the approaching struggle ?

Ramon (*shaking his head slowly*). I have heard no news as yet, Senor. I came in to tell you the material has just arrived for the new outhouses. The carrier has also just arrived with the letters and papers from the city of Santiago.

James (*throwing down pen and rising*).   Ah, the papers are what I want.   Is there anything about the finding of the board of inquiry concerning the destruction of the American battle-ship " Maine."

Ramon (*shaking his head*).   Nothing so far, Señor Crawford. However all the search in the world will only prove the ship met with an accident.   That the explosion came from the inside of the boat and not from any torpedo hidden in the water will be easily proved.   (*Quickly.*)   But why is the señor so anxious to find out ?

James (*proudly*).   Because I am an American, and the men killed in the darkness of the night were also Americans ! (*Sternly.*)   And if the Spanish government had anything to do with this despicable plot, it will receive a lesson it will never forget.   [**Exit** L., *quickly.*

Ramon (*looking after him and then with a sneer*).   So the Spanish will receive a lesson they will never forget, eh ?   Just like all Americans !   You think your own country the greatest on earth.   (*Warningly.*)   But beware, Señor Crawford !   Don't trifle with the Spanish, or you may learn that you have gone too far before we get through with you !   (*Savagely.*)   Curse you, James Crawford, how I hate you !   You little knew who I was when I applied for the position of overseer of the plantation and what motive I had in doing so.   (*Shaking his fist after him.*) But you will in time, never fear, you will in time.

[LOUIS **enters** *from* C. *smoking.*

Louis (*blowing a cloud of smoke in the air*).   Well, father, what devilment are you up to now ?   You have a look on your face that would shake the American continent from shore to shore.

Ramon (*looking around in alarm and then speaking in a whisper*).   You fool !   How many times must I tell you not to call me father ?   Especially while you are under this roof. Someone might hear you, and then all my scheming would be in vain.   (*Grasping him by the arm and looking around.*) While you are in this house, we must not be known as father and son.   Understand that in future, Louis.

Louis (*nodding his head slowly*).   You are quite right. (*Quickly.*)   But will you kindly let me know what kind of a game you are playing, so that in future I may be on my guard.

Ramon (*thoughtfully*).   I don't know as it will do you much good to know.   Still in future you will be prepared not to make a mess of it by your rashness.

Louis.   Then let me know at once.   As the Yankees say, I am dying to find out.

Ramon.   Years ago, while in New York, I accidentally met one of the handsomest girls I ever laid my eyes on.   We were introduced to each other, and it seemed to be a case of love at first sight—at least it was on my side.

Louis (*laughing*). So it seems you were susceptible to female loveliness, after all, eh ?

Ramon (*coldly*). You think it strange that the man you call by the name of father never felt the tender pangs of love. (*Quickly.*) Boy, this girl was a perfect angel, if there ever was one on earth. Yes, Louis, I have felt the pierce of Cupid's dart.

Louis (*laughing*). I suppose you must have, or I would not be here at the present time.

Ramon (*sternly*). Young man, your mother I honored and respected, but never loved.

Louis (*in amazement*). The deuce you didn't !

Ramon (*sneering*). It surprises you, does it ?

Louis (*nodding his head slowly*). Well, rather.

Ramon. You will find out a great many more things that will surprise you, when you come to know me better, my dear son, Louis.

Louis (*laughing*). I haven't the slightest doubt of it. But continue with the story you commenced.

Ramon. Very well. Pay strict attention to what I am saying and you will then know why I hate this Yankee dog as I do !

Louis (*looking around*). Hurry up, then, before someone comes along and interrupts us.

Ramon. Listen then. I proposed to this young woman and was most politely refused. My rank as a Spanish nobleman had no attraction for her.

Louis. Hem !

Ramon. Yes, refused me. I, Don Ramon Marana, of Castile, son of one of Spain's greatest noblemen, for the sake of a low down American dog, without the semblance of a title. (*Savagely.*) And do you know why I was refused ? Do you know, I say ?

Louis (*shaking his head slowly*). I haven't the slightest idea, I am sure. Perhaps, the young lady loved the American better than she did you.

Ramon (*slowly*). You are right, Louis. The fair American girl did love some one else better, and that some one was James Crawford.

Louis (*in amazement*). James Crawford !

Ramon. You are surprised, eh ?

Louis (*nodding*). Well, rather.

Ramon. I swore to be revenged on him for marrying the only woman I ever loved ! But the American is a sly devil, and has baffled me so far. The wife died in giving birth to Alma. I lost track of them for years and only recently discovered them living in Cuba. The flame of my vengeance has been smoulder-

ing all these years, but has never entirely died out.   I happened
to be in this neighborhood when he advertised for an overseer
for his plantation, and I determined to cast my rank to the winds
and accept a position in his house.   I applied for the position
and was accepted.

Louis.   And were you not afraid he would recognize you ?

Ramon (*shaking his head slowly*).   Not at all, my son.
While the years have dealt kindly with him they have made
many changes in me.

Louis.   And what do you intend to do ?

Ramon.   That you shall hear now.   In the first place you
shall marry the girl at all hazards.

Louis.   And what if she refuses ?

Ramon (*sternly*).   Marry her anyway !   The day for the
completion of my revenge is close at hand.   The destruction of
the American battleship " Maine " was the first step in the
right direction.   In a short time from now it will be Don
Ramon Marana, who will be proprietor of these vast estates,
and James Crawford the slave !   (*Listening ; then quickly.*)
Someone is coming.   It will never do for the two of us to be
seen together, as it may excite suspicion.   So for the present,
my son, I will leave you.   [**Exit** L. *quickly.*

Louis (*looking after him*).   So, my respected father, that is
why you are humbling yourself at the present time.   You may
be a smart man, but I am afraid you will find your match in
the American James Crawford.   [**Exit** L., *puffing his cigar.*

DENNIS **enters** *from* C.

Dennis (*looking around in surprise*).   Shure, there's no wan
in the room at all, at all.   I was positive I heard some wan
talkin' in this room just before I entered.   An' it seemed to me
as if wan ov thim was the new overseer.   There is somethin'
strange about that divil I don't understand.   He claims to be a
Cuban, but he seems more like a Spaniard to me.   Whoever
was in the room was using tobacco, for I can smell the smoke.

INEZ **enters** *from* L.

Inez (*in surprise*).   Señor Rafferty !

Dennis (*bowing*).   Acushla !   (*Aside.*)   Be heavens, that's
Irish an' not Spanish !   (*Aloud.*)   Señorita, why do you always
call me Señor Rafferty ?   Why don't you call me plain Dennis
like all the rest av thim.

Inez (*sitting on sofa*).   The señor forgets I am a Cuban girl.
To speak to the señor like that would make me-his equal.   Such
I am not at the present time.   The Cubans are now fighting for
their liberty.   We are treated simply as slaves by the Spanish
government.

Dennis (*sitting on the side of desk*). You just show me the Spanish galoot that treats you as a slave, an' I'll just take an' kick the divilment out av him! (*Aside.*) Now to make an impression on her. (*Aloud.*) You know I am a good man whin it comes to a fight. I am afraid of nothing.

Inez (*smiling*). How brave you are, Señor.

Dennis (*aside*). I'll have her yet. I'll have her yet! (*Aloud.*) But, señorita, haven't you iver thought av gittin' married? (*Aside.*) Now to git mushy. (*Aloud.*) Haven't ye iver felt the tinder pangs av love's young drame?

Inez (*sighing*). Love!

Dennis (*nodding*). Yis, fair creature, love! (*Aside.*) I'll win her this time if that divil av a nagur will only kape away until I can pop the question.

Inez. And what is love, Señor Rafferty?

Dennis (*aside*). I wonder is this Cuban girl stringin' av me. (*Aloud.*) Love, me darlin', is whin ye have such a feelin' for another person that ye can't do without him.

[SAM *runs in from* C. *and remains standing in the doorway, with a smile on his face, and unseen by either one of the others.*

Sam (*grinning*). Hi! the I'ishman, am makin' love agin. I'll have some fun with the two of them.

[**Exit** *door* C., *but peeps in from time to time.*

Inez. (*holding down her head*). And has the Señor Rafferty ever felt like that?

Dennis (*aside*). Lots av times before. (*Aloud.*) Niver until I saw you, me fair señorita.

Inez (*archly*). And you are sure you love me, then?

Dennis (*shaking his head quickly*). I am that. (*Aside.*) She's mine this time.

Inez. But the man I marry must fight for my country, for the liberty of Cuba.

Dennis (*quickly*). Faith, I'll fight for it five times, if wance ain't enough, if you'll promise to be me own true lovin' little wife.

Sam (*looking in*). Everythin' am cert'nly workin' in the I'ishman's favor this time. I'll have to get my work in before I'm too late.

Dennis. Well, me darlin'; I'm waitin'. (*Crosses to* L.)

Sam (*looking in and mewing like a cat*). Miaw!

Inez (*jumping up in alarm*). Oh, Señor Rafferty, what a horrible sound.

Dennis (*looking around the room*). Sh! it sounds to me like the dying wail av a managerie.

[SAM *looks in, grins, and then mews again.*

Inez. Mercy! The room must be haunted! (*Runs out* L.)

Dennis *(looking around the room closely).* I knew we had cats on the plantation, but I never knew before they were as big as tigers. The cat that gave that last cry must be the size av an elephant.   [SAM *looks in and then mews again.*

Dennis *(jumping around in affright).* Be heavens, I thought he was on me shoulders that time. *(Goes down on his hands and knees and begins to search.)* I'll find him this time if he's in the room. *(SAM pokes his head in and mews just as DEN-NIS looks up and catches him.)* Ah, ah, nagur, so you were the cause av the disturbance, eh? *(Jumping up.)*

SAM **enters** *from* C.

Sam *(laughing).* I'ishman don't get mad.

Dennis. Nagur, do you know what I have a mind to do with you?

Sam *(shaking his head).* Don't know, sah.

Dennis. I have a good mind to break yer head. *(He doubles up and shakes his fist at SAM.)*

Sam *(looking away from him).* White man, yo' git funny w'th me an' I'll cert'nly ha'm yo' bad. Yo' he'h me speakin' now, white man.

Dennis *(making a face at him).* Go on, you nagur.

Sam *(making face at DENNIS).* Go on, yo' no 'count I'ishman. Yo' ain't even got a country of yo' own.

Dennis *(in amazement).* Well, well, would ye listen to that now! An' I suppose you have?

Sam *(proudly).* Yes, sah, the greatest on the face of the earth!

Dennis *(in surprise).* Oh, have you now? An' shure what may the name av it be? Africa, where all the monkeys come from?

Sam *(shaking his head).* No, sah, America!

Dennis *(aside).* I'd a murdered him if he said Ireland! *(Aloud.)* Well, well! An' do you call yourself an American? An' would ye mind tellin' me what part av America ye call home?

Sam *(proudly).* Virginia, sah!

Dennis *(laughing).* Shure, whin did they ship Thompson Street, New York, down to Virginia?

Sam. I'ishman', yo' am a liar!

Dennis. You're a black gorilla, nagur! *(Both clinch and begin to struggle.)*

ALMA **enters** *from* C.

Alma *(in surprise).* Why Sam, Dennis, what does this mean? I am really surprised! What is the meaning of this scene?

[At sound of her voice both separate and look rather foolish ; SAM *stands at door* L. *making motions for* DENNIS *to say something.*

Dennis (*humbly*).   Shure we were just tryin' to settle a little dispute bechune us.

Alma (*nodding*).   Oh, I see! (*Laughing.*) Fighting as usual. Sam, return to your work.

Sam (*bowing humbly*).   Yes, missis Alma.

[**Exit** L., *after making a face at* DENNIS.

Alma.   And now, Dennis, I wish to speak to you. (*In a whisper.*) I know I can depend on you.

Dennis (*earnestly*).   Shure, I'd lay down my life to help you if it would do any good !

Alma (*gratefully*).   Thank you, Dennis ! (*Looks around cautiously.*) I want you to keep an eye on this new overseer that my father has engaged.   Since the trouble between America and Spain commenced it seems to me his actions are rather suspicious than otherwise.   I am afraid he is not as loyal to the Cuban cause as he pretends.

Dennis (*nodding*).   I'll kape an eye on him, niver fear.   An' if the divil tries to git funny with me it will be all up with him.

[**Exit** L.

Alma (*looking after him*).   Faithful friends ! (*Sits on sofa.*) All the time quarrelling, and yet the best of friends at all times. This home would indeed be lonesome if it wasn't for the two of them. (*Quickly.*) Ah, I had quite forgotten Robert. (*Thoughtfully.*) I wonder does he ever think of me in the same way as I do of him. (*Shaking her head slowly.*) I am afraid not.

ROBERT **enters** *from* C.

Robert (*quickly advancing towards* ALMA).   Miss Alma, can I speak to you for a moment on a very serious question ? I won't detain you but a moment.

Alma (*rising in surprise*).   Why, certainly you can.   But you seem to be excited.

Robert (*nodding his head quickly*).   And I have good cause to be.

Alma.   What do you mean, Robert ?

Robert (*slowly*).   I mean I am going to quit the employment of your father !

Alma (*in amazement*).   You are going to leave my father ! And why are you going to leave us, Robert ?

Robert.   Because my first duty is towards my country ! I am going to fight for the honor of the stars and stripes ! I am going to help avenge the brave sailors who perished in the destruction of the " Maine." Their blood cries to heaven for vengeance ! It is the duty of every patriotic American citizen to shoulder a gun in the coming struggle !

Alma (*in surprise*). But war has not been declared yet ! It may all pass off peaceably enough.

Robert (*shaking his head quickly*). You are wrong, Alma. There is nothing left for the Spanish nation to do but acknowledge they destroyed the "Maine," or fight ! The former they will never do, the latter they must do ! I wouldn't be surprised to hear that war was declared between Spain and America inside of twenty-four hours. I am going to leave for New York at once. But before I go I wish to speak to you about something that concerns me very deeply.

Alma (*quietly*). I am all attention, Robert.

Robert. You and I have known each other for a number of years. The more I have seen of you, the better I have liked you, until this liking has turned into love. I am leaving now and may never return again. But before I go I wish to hear from your own lips what my fate is going to be. If you say yes, I can face the enemy with the satisfaction that some one is waiting for my safe return. And now, Alma, you have heard my confession. I love you truly and want you to be my wife. What is your answer going to be ?

Alma (*bashfully*). Here is my answer, Robert. (*She places arms around his neck and kisses him.*) I will be your wife whenever you want me.

Robert (*in delight*). You mean it, Alma ?

Alma. Yes, Robert, I do.

Robert. Then the war can't come any too soon for me. Let us go and see what your father has got to say about the matter.

Alma (*laughing*). With all my heart.

[*Both* **exeunt** *hand-in-hand.*

LOUIS **enters** *from* L.

Louis (*looking around*). I thought perhaps I might be able to see the fair American senorita. I must find how I stand in the game of love with the young woman. If I could only get the damned young American out of my way, I would stand a better show of winning his fair countrywoman !

JAMES **enters** *from* L.

James (*quietly*). Well, Señor Marana, I am afraid it's all up. War is sure to be declared, and then it will be all up with Cuba as a Spanish possession.

Louis (*slowly*). You mean that Cuba will be freed ?

James. Yes, and in a hurry !

Louis. Perhaps not. Remember the Spanish nation can fight !

James (*laughing*). They won't think so when the boys of Uncle Sam get through with them !

Louis (*aside*). You cursed American dog ! (*Aloud.*) Let us hope it won't come to the worst, Señor Crawford. And now that we are face to face there is something I wish to say to you.

James (*quietly*). Well, sir ?

Louis. It's something that concerns your daughter and myself very deeply. I love her and wish to make her my wife !

James (*slowly*). Well, Señor, I never interfere in the happiness of my daughter in any manner whatsoever. What answer did she make to your declaration of love ?

Louis (*slowly*). You will pardon me, Señor, but I have not yet spoken to your daughter on the subject.

James (*laughing*). So you believe in speaking to the father first ?

Louis (*nodding*). Yes, Señor, I do.

James. I will send for my daughter and hear what she has to say for herself.

[*She overhears his last words as she enters.*

ALMA enters *from* C.

Alma. I am here to answer for myself, father. What is it you wish to know of me ?

James (*pointing to* LOUIS). This gentleman will tell you himself. Speak up, young man, and don't be afraid.

Louis. Señorita Crawford, I have just asked your hand in marriage from your father.

James (*quietly*). You have heard the question, Alma, and can now answer for yourself.

Alma (*slowly*). I am very sorry, father, but I am forced to decline his kind offer. I am the promised wife of another.

Louis (*quickly*). You have promised to marry Señor Hamilton ?

Alma (*bowing*). I have.

Louis (*furiously*). And so you prefer the love of this American pauper to that of a Spanish nobleman ?

James (*in amazement*). A Spanish nobleman ? Then you are not a Cuban as you pretended ?

Louis (*in disgust*). A Cuban ! The Cubans are all black. I am a white man ! My father is one of the great men of Spain.

ROBERT enters *from* C.

Robert (*holding up a paper*). Glad news ! War has been declared between Spain and the United States ! A call has been issued for volunteers !

James. And are you going to enlist, Robert ?

Robert. You bet I am, and fight like a demon for the stars and stripes !

Louis (*savagely*). Curse the stars and stripes ! Thus do we of Spain treat the boastful flag of America !

[*He tears down the flag from the wall, throws it on the floor and stamps on it.*

Robert (*quickly*). Take that, you Spanish dog !

[*He strikes him with his fist and knocks him down.*

Alma (*in alarm*). Oh, Robert, what have you done ?

[*Places hand on his arm.*

Robert (*fearlessly*). Struck the first blow for the freedom of Cuba and the honor of America !

[*Picks up flag and wraps it around her shoulders.* ALMA *and* ROBERT C. ; LOUIS *lying on the floor* L. ; JAMES *standing* R.

SLOW CURTAIN.

ACT II.

SCENE.—*A deep wood, full depth of stage. Wood wings and borders ; grass carpet down ; a number of guns are stacked down* R. ; *the stump of an old tree down* L., *used for a seat ; lights half down. Running from* R. 4 E. *to* L. 4 E. *is a wall of brush three feet high ; the flat shows a continuation of the woods in the distance. Music " The girl I left behind me."*

DENNIS *is standing* R. *looking at the guns as the curtain rises.* ROBERT **enters** *from* L.

Robert (*laughing*). Well, Sergeant Rafferty, do you think any of the guns managed to escape ?

Dennis (*turning around at sound of the voice and then saluting*). I was only thinkin' how many Spanish lives aich wan av thim guns contained. (*Quickly.*) But thin the dirty skunks won't show thimselves so that wan av our min can raich thim with a bullet !

Robert (*nodding his head slowly*). You are quite right, Rafferty. The Spanish may be great bull-fighters, and all that, but when it comes man to man and gun to gun, they are away out of reach.

[*Sits down* L. ; *takes a cigar from pocket, lights same and begins to smoke.*

Dennis (*throwing himself on the ground*). Thrue for ye, sur. So long as they can jab a knife in yer back, or run it across yer neck whin yer not lukin', they are a mighty brave lot av min, an' no mistake.

[*While he is speaking he has been filling a pipe which he now lights and begins to puff.*

Robert. So it seems, Dennis. But I am afraid they have met their match at last in the brave boys of Uncle Sam !

Dennis (*puffing at his pipe and then blowing a cloud of smoke in the air*). We'd make short wurk av the divils if they would only come out an' show thimselves like min. (*In disgust.*) This blashted bush fightin' is somethin' I don't like at all ! Wan minute up to yer neck in wather an' the next almost killed be the heat av the sun !

Robert (*laughing*). Have no fear, Dennis, most of the "Rough Riders," are cowboys from the West, and well used to all kinds of weather and especially this kind of fighting. Mark my words, it will only be a short time before Santiago falls into the hands of the American soldiers !

Dennis. An' heaven help the residents once the Cuban insurgents are allowed to take possession of the city. The wild half starved fellows will make short wurk av the garrison an' the city itself, I am afraid.

Robert. That is something General Shafter will not allow. The Spanish garrison need have no fear in surrendering. The Americans will see they are well protected from the fury of the Cuban insurgents. I am afraid the Spanish are going to pay dearly for the destruction of the "Maine" before we get through with them. They will never want to repeat the trick again !

Dennis (*indignantly*). Serves them right, the cowardly dogs, if they lost all their possessions. It may teach them a lesson, an' do thim good !

Robert. If I only knew for a certainty that Alma and her father were safe, I would not worry as I do. But since I have learned that Louis Marana has become an officer in the Spanish garrison at Santiago, my fears for their safety have redoubled. I am almost driven wild with anxiety about my darling Alma ! To have her exposed to the tender mercy of such a man as Marana, is something awful to contemplate !

Dennis. Have no fear, sir. All will yet end well. Bad as the devil is, he wouldn't dare to harm her, I am sure. He loves her too dearly.

Robert (*sternly*). Curse him, if he offered any harm to Alma, I would follow him even to Spain, to wreak my vengeance on his cowardly head ! (*Quickly.*) But, Dennis, you had better go and learn when the next step in the direction of Santiago is to be made.

Dennis (*rising and saluting*). Very well, captain. I'll be back as soon as I can. [**Exit** R.

Robert (*thoughtfully*). What a strange world we are living in. Six months ago, who would ever have supposed that the peaceful people of a country like America would be plunged into a war with another nation. And yet, strange as it may seem, Spain is the very country that advanced the money and ships to discover the American continent. Perhaps, after all the war may be the biggest kind of a benefit to the Spanish nation. Once soundly whipped and her days of underhand dealing may come to an end. So far, all is in the hands of God who rules the universe as He sees fit. If America is to win, America will win in spite of all the soldiers in Spain! ·

PEDRO enters *from* R. 4 E.

Pedro (*looks around cautiously and then comes down to* ROBERT *and speaks in a whisper after making an awkward salute*). Señor Captain, can I speak to you a moment?

Robert (*in surprise*). Well, sir, who are you, and what do you want? Speak up, man.

Pedro (*humbly*). I am known as Pedro, señor.

Robert (*quickly*). Ah, yes, you are one of the insurgents we picked up on our way here.

Pedro. Si, señor. But I am more than the simple insurgent you think I am. (*Looking around and then in a whisper.*) I am Pedro, the Cuban spy—the terror of the Spanish army!

Robert. Not the same Pedro, the spy, the American soldiers have heard so much about?

Pedro (*bowing*). The same, señor.

Robert. Well, Pedro, I am glad you are among us, as you can be of great help to us at the present. But why do you come to me? Have you news for me?

Pedro. Si, señor.

Robert. Then out with it at once.

Pedro. I have been in the city of Santiago less than three days ago. One determined assault and the city will fall. The soldiers will surrender willingly to the Americans, as it means their deliverance from death by starvation. They are without ammunition or provisions of any kind.

Robert (*laughing*). Well, if the fools will try and hold out against us, then they have no one to blame but themselves.

Pedro (*looking around*). But, señor, on my way back here I passed the plantation of the rich American, Señor Crawford.

Robert (*eagerly*). And are they all well?

Pedro. Si, señor. Most of the cattle and provisions have been stolen by the Spanish soldiers.

Robert. And did you see the young lady?

Pedro (*nodding*). Si, señor. And she gave me this letter for you. (*He takes a letter from his breast which he hands to* ROBERT.) And, now, señor, I must leave you. But before I go, I wish to tell you to keep an eye on three of the Cubans in the camp at the present time. I do not know them. Still that is not strange, as we are not all known to one another, although fighting for the same cause. So keep an eye on them. And now, señor, for the present, *adios.* In case you should want me, señor, to send an answer to the letter, you will find me among some of the insurgents, *adios.* [**Exit** R., *quickly.*

Robert (*looking at letter*). Only to think that for the first time since the war commenced, I am to hear from my own little sweetheart. Let me see what she has to say. (*He opens envelope and takes out sheet of paper which he opens and then reads aloud.*) "My darling Robert, you don't know how delighted I am to hear that you and your gallant comrades have landed on the soil of Cuba safe and sound, and will not leave again until the stars and stripes shall float in triumph over this down-trodden country as a free nation! The bearer of this letter is a noted Cuban spy and may be relied on ; so don't be afraid to trust him. My father and I have made arrangements with him to conduct us to your camp, if you will allow us to visit you. He declares there is no harm in venturing to the trenches, as hostilities will not commence again for some time. I am fairly dying to see you once more. It may be for the last time. If you will permit me to visit the camp, just tell the spy and he will conduct me to you without delay. Please don't refuse me this time. I am yours lovingly until death do us part, Alma Crawford!" (*Rising and folding letter he places same in envelope and places it in his breast.*) By George, she is right! We can't advance any further for the present at least. And, as she says, it may be the last time we shall ever meet again. A Spanish bullet is just as liable to kill me as any of my comrades. I'll hunt up the spy and have him bring Alma and her father to the camp without delay. It will be like old times to catch one glimpse of my darling's beautiful smiling face. Life in camp won't be so lonely to me when I hear from the lips of my future wife that she is still true to her fighting American soldier boy. (*Quickly.*) In the meantime I must not forget the advice the spy gave me about keeping an eye on the strange insurgents in the camp. Now to find Pedro. [**Exit** R.

SAM **enters** *from* L.

Sam (*he is carrying a pail of water and wiping his face with the back of his hand as he enters*). Whew! The weather am cut'nly wa'm. (*He places pail on the ground beside the seat* L.) My lan'! I nevah did see no such weatha in America nohow! A niggah am supposed to love the wa'm weather, but this am cut'nly a little too wa'm for this chile. I wondah where am the I'ishman? [*Looks around.*

DENNIS enters *from* R.

Dennis. Well, nagur, what are you doin' there ?

Sam (*fanning himself with his hat*). Trying to keep cool, white man, tryin' to keep cool.

Dennis. An' shure what have ye in the pail, may I ax ?
[*He points to pail as he speaks.*

Sam. That am water fo' massa Robert to drink, yo' fool white man. Yo' tink I'm ca'in' watah fo' fun ?

Dennis. Nagur, whatever ye do don't git funny with the army. Ye are shure to git in throuble.

Sam (*making a motion with his hand as if chasing a chicken*). Shoo, white man, shoo !

Dennis. Nagur, ye are not huntin' for chickens now, so shtop wurkin' yer hands.

Sam. I do cut'nly wish I could lay my hands on a good fat chicken now. (*Smacking his lips.*) Lud, white man, I'd fry him, feathers and all !

Dennis. For heaven's sake, nagur, don't ye git enough to ate ?

Sam. I cut'nly does, white man ; but yo' nevah heard of an army being fed on chicken, did ye ?

Dennis (*shaking his head and laughing*). Not if they didn't steal them, nagur.

[*The sound of a rooster crowing is heard from off* L. *quite faintly.*

Sam (*quickly ; listening*). What am that, I'ish ?

Dennis (*listening*). Sounded like chickens, or I am a liar.

[*Both listen ; the sound is repeated again but much nearer than before.*

Sam (*excitedly*). It am chickens, an' I am going to git one of them or die in the 'tempt.   [*Runs out* L.

Dennis (*quickly*). Thin, be heavens, if ye are, ye won't have it all to yerself, if I can help it !

[*Runs out* L. *in close pursuit of* SAM.

LOUIS enters *from* R. 4 E. *followed by two men disguised as Cuban insurgents.*

Louis (*looking around in a cautious manner and then speaking in a whisper*). Now, then, men, listen carefully to what I am going to say. (*Both men nod and bend close to hear what he has to say.*) This is the camp and headquarters of the American, Hamilton. Now here is the plan laid out before us. By playing our cards well failure is impossible. And if we do fail you know what will become of us. (*Both nod.*) Now, then. (*He takes a small bottle from his pocket and holds it up for them to see.*) A few drops of the liquid contained in this bottle placed in this water will render whoever drinks of the same unconscious for a number of hours. My object is to capture the American captain and carry him back with us to Santiago as a prisoner. At a given signal you will fire a number of shots off yonder. (*Points off* L.) That will put the Americans on their guard to repulse a sudden attack from the enemy. During the excitement we will hurry away with the American officer through a secret path I have discovered in the woods. When he recovers his senses he will be a prisoner in Santiago. Our only hope is to have him drink of the water. (*He empties the bottle into the pail of water.*) Away, now, and be ready to do my bidding. (*Both* exeunt R. 4 E.) And now, Señor Hamilton, we will see if, when once you are in my power, with no chance of escape, the haughty American señorita will not promise to be my wife in order to save your life ! One swallow of the water and you are dead to the world for a number of hours.   [**Exit** R. 4 E.

ROBERT enters *from* L.

Robert (*looking at his watch*). According to what this Cuban spy tells me, he should be here in a short time from now with Alma and her father. I am so anxious that every minute seems an age to me. Perhaps I am too impatient altogether. He said it would take him less than an hour to go and come, and the time is almost up now. (*Looks off* R.) As I live, here they come now.

ALMA *and her father* enter *from* R.

Alma (*rushing into* ROBERT'S *arms*). Oh, Robert, only to think that we have the happiness of meeting once more ! I was so afraid we should never see each other again.

Robert (*kissing her passionately*). Have no fear, darling. The Spanish soldiers will have to shoot a great deal straighter than they do if they wish to kill any of the men from the American army !

James (*who has been up* C. *examining the brush wall, now comes down to where they are standing*). Yes, but they are not in the habit of trying to shoot straight when they can accomplish just as much without any danger to themselves. For instance, just take the case of the battleship " Maine."

Robert (*quickly*). Which Admiral Dewey nobly avenged by sinking the Spanish fleet of Admiral Montejo in the bay of Manila ! And heaven only knows what Sampson will do with the fleet of Admiral Cervera if he can only once get a crack at him !

James (*thoughtfully*). What do you mean by Dewey and the bay of Manila ? (*Quickly.*) Do you mean the American fleet was victorious ?

Robert (*nodding*).   Certainly I do !   Montejo's entire Spanish fleet is now at the bottom of Manila Bay !   The same fate that befell the Spanish navy in the waters of the Philippines also awaits the ships of Spain in this part of the world !

James (*in amazement*).   Well, well, you surprise me, Robert. There was great rejoicing among the people of Santiago over the brilliant victory of the Spanish admiral and the destruction of the American fleet.

Robert (*laughing*).   That is but a sample of the news the Spanish are sending out.   If the truth were known the soldiers of Spain in the garrison of Santiago would throw down their arms and refuse to fight longer.

Alma.   Father, hadn't you better tell the news to Robert ? As we have been receiving false news from the outside, why may not the news of what has been happening on the island be withheld from the Americans ?

Robert (*in surprise*).   What do you mean, Alma ?

Alma.   Father will tell you all.

James.   Listen, Robert, and I will tell you.

Robert (*bowing*).   Very well, sir, I am all attention.

Alma.   Pay particular attention to what father is saying, and when he gets through I am sure you will be just the least bit surprised.

Robert.   Proceed, Mr. Crawford.

James.   You remember the overseer I had on my plantation before the war commenced ?

Robert.   Certainly.   He was a red-hot Cuban sympathizer.

James (*nodding*).   So he led us all to believe.   But it turned out he was no Cuban, but a Spanish nobleman masquerading as a Cuban, and the father of your old enemy Captain Louis Marana.

Robert.   And what object had he in masquerading thus ?

James (*shaking his head*).   That is more than I can say. At the present time Ramon Marana is one of the head men of the city of Santiago, and his word is law.

LOUIS **enters** *from* R. 4 E., *stops on seeing the others, shakes his fist at them, and then* **exit** *again.*

Robert (*in amazement*).   Well, well, I must say that I am more than surprised !   I am simply astonished !

PEDRO *runs in from* L.

James.   Well, Pedro, what is the matter ?   You seem to be excited ?

Pedro.   I think the American señor and his fair daughter had better leave the camp at once.

James.   Do you mean that danger threatens us ?

Pedro. I am afraid so, señor.

Robert. What is the danger, Pedro ?

Pedro. I am unable to say, señor. But I am afraid the Spanish mean to make a combined attack on the camp. There will be much danger for the girl if she remains.

Alma. Perhaps he is right, Robert. We had better return at once. By remaining we would only be in your way, and thus be an obstacle in the way of your success.

Robert. Very well, Alma. (*He embraces and kisses her, and then shakes hands with her father.*) And now, Pedro, conduct them in safety from the camp.

Pedro. You can trust me, señor.

[**Exit** L. *followed by* ALMA *and her father.*

Robert (*looking after them*). Dear girl ! If anything should happen to her, I wouldn't care how soon a Spanish bullet would put an end to my life ! (*He sits down* L.) How warm it is growing !

LOUIS **enters** *from* R. 4 E. *followed by one of his men, and both stand watching.*

Robert. The heat of Cuba is something fearful. (*Looks around and sees a pail of water.*) Ah, faithful Sam ! Always looking after my comfort and welfare ! Who else would have the presence of mind to furnish me with such a pail of clear, cool, sparkling water. (*He takes a cupfull and drinks it.*) How strange it tastes. (*He drinks another.*) What is the matter with me ?

[*The cup falls from his hands, he sways for a moment when* LOUIS *crosses quickly from* R. *and catches him just as he is about to fall to the ground.*

Louis (*holding him in his arms, motions for his companion to help him ; the latter crosses from* R. *and takes hold of* ROBERT'S *lifeless form.*) Quick ! The drug has done its work !

[*They lift* ROBERT *between them and carry him out* R., *leaving his hat on the ground beside the pail of water; a number of shots are heard from off* L. *followed by a volley and then a cheer.*

DENNIS **enters** *from* L. *followed by* SAM, *who has a chicken in each hand.*

Dennis (*calling*). Captain, captain, where are you, I say ? (*He looks around.*)

Sam (*pointing to hat on ground with his foot.*) What am that, l'ish ?

Dennis (*picking it up*). Shure, it's Robert's hat ? What can have become of him ?

Sam (*excitedly looking off* R.). The Lord save us ! There goes two men in the distance, an' they have the captain 'tween 'em, suah !

Dennis. The Spanish divils have made a prisoner of him ! But we'll save the life av Robert, or die in the attempt !

[*He raises right hand towards Heaven.*

Sam. 'Deed we will, I'ish !

[*He raises right hand with the chicken still held in it.*

SLOW CURTAIN.

ACT III.

Scene.—*Interior of a stone block house. Door* C., *small door* R., *window* L., *covered with iron bars ; small table and stool down* L.   ROBERT *is chained to the wall* R. C. ; JAMES *is lying on a heap of straw down* R., *asleep, and chained to the floor. Music.*

Robert (*struggling with his chains*). It's no use. I have tried over and over again to break the links, but they are too strong for me. It's no use. I may as well save my strength ! What can be the meaning ot all this ? How came I to be in this strong place ? I remember parting with Alma and her father in the camp, and then what happened ? (*Quickly.*) Ah, yes ! I remember feeling overcome with the heat and sitting down. And then what ? Yes, yes, the water ! That was it ! The water I drank ! It must have been drugged. I remember drinking the second cup, and then I remember nothing more. When I came to I found myself in this room with Mr. Crawford as my companion, and the both of us chained up like dogs. I wonder are we quite near Santiago ? If so we can't be very far from the camp of the boys of Uncle Sam, and the guns of Sampson will make short work of this place once they are set in motion. Whoever had a hand in this dirty piece of work will pay dearly if I can lay my hands on them. It's bad enough to be a prisoner, but to be chained up like a dog is something I can't bear to think of. And we free-born citizens of the grand and glorious United States of America ! If Louis Marana or his father had anything to do with this work there will be an awful account to settle between us when once I am free.

[*The face of* SAM *appears at window. He has on a Spanish soldier's coat and cap, and a gun over his shoulder.*

Sam (*looking around cautiously before he speaks, and then in a whisper*). Massa Robert! oh, Massa!

Robert (*looking towards window in surprise*). Why, it can't be—yes, it's Sam! Why, Sam, old fellow, how came you here?

Sam (*whispering*). Not so loud, massa. Someone might hear yo', an' then all the fat would be in the fire, fo' suah.

Robert (*whispering*). Trust me, Sam. I will be very careful. The sight of your welcome face caused me to speak louder than I intended to. But you haven't answered my question yet. What does it all mean?

Sam. Listen, then, fo' I haven't got no time to fool 'round heah.

Robert (*quickly*). Have no fear, Sam. I'll promise to pay particular attention to what you are going to say. Only try and explain this awful mystery to me. Tell me, Sam, for God's sake, how I came to be chained up in this hole like a dog! It's all such a deep, dark mystery to me!

Sam. Myself an' Massa Pedro tracked yo' to this place. We lay in wait an' when we had a good chance made a prisoner of the guard. He showed fight, but he won't no mo'.

Robert (*in amazement*). You don't mean you killed him?

Sam (*shaking his head*). No, sah! Pedro finished him pretty quick, I can tell yo'.

Robert. Horrible!

Sam. I know dat, sah! But den Pedro am a Cuban an' he was a Spaniard, so that makes um all right.

Robert. I hope so, Sam. But go on.

Sam. Den I took his clothes an' gun an' played guard myself, sah.

Robert. But you haven't told me yet how I came to be here along with Mr. Crawford, and how you came to discover us.

Sam. I'll jess tell yo' in a minute, sah. Dis mo'ning when the sudden 'tack came, we couldn't find yo' nohow. We found yo' hat aftah hunting all over. Den we saw two men ca'ying yo' away with them. We was afraid to chase aftah yo' on 'count Spanish bullets. We had to wait until Pedro came an' den tell him what happened. He swore at fust an' den he went hunting all through the camp. We all thought him crazy at fust, until he told us three of the Cubans had disappeared. We all looked fo' them, sah, but dey was gone fo' suah. Jess den one of de men took a drink from the pail of watah, an' him jess fell ovah an' we all thinks him dead! The doctah examined the man an' sed he didn't know what was the mattah with him. Den he thinks ob the watah, an' aftah tasting it he say it am drugged.

Robert. And so it was. And then what?

Sam. And then Pedro determined to hunt yo' up if he possibly could. So we started out to track your captors and yo'self.

Robert. Wasn't that rather risky, Sam ?

Sam. Shuah it was. But den I is an' American, sah, an' I am not afraid of anything.

Robert (*laughing*). Good for you, Sam. But have you any idea who it was that brought us here ?

Sam (*nodding*). I know dat, too, sah.

Robert. You do, Sam ?

Sam. Yes, sah. Yo' remember the three strange Cubans we had in the camp this mo'ning ?

Robert. Certainly.

Sam. One of them was Louis Marana, the Spanish cap'n, and the others two of his men in disguise.

Robert (*aside*). Just as I thought. (*Aloud.*) How do you know that, Sam ?

Sam. Pedro found um all out.

Robert. What could have been his object ?

Sam (*shaking his head*). I dunno, sah. What troubles me am Massa Crawford dead or only jess sleeping. He ain't moved since I been here.

Robert. He is not dead, Sam. As he was captured later than I he is still under the influence of some drug. But, Sam, won't you try and help us out of this scrape ? Help us to regain our liberty.

Sam. Why, cert'nly, sah, that is why I am here. Can't help you now, sah, must wait 'til da'k.

Robert. I'm afraid it will then be too late !

Sam. Well, sah, if yo' am going only jess remembah I am heah to die with yo' sah. I must leave yo' now, sah, an' play the part of the guard befo' I am discovered to be an American nigger, sah. But remembah, if the wust comes to the wust, I'll put a chunk of lead into some one for the sake of the Union and Old Glory ! [*Disappears from the window.*

Robert. So Louis Marana is the cause of my present misfortune, is he ? Like all of the Spanish dogs, he won't face me man to man ! But the time will come when we shall meet, and it will be the last time on this side of the grave. (*Wildly.*) Great God ! To think that my peerless Alma may at this moment be in the clutches of this monster, almost drives me wild ! Oh, woe to you Louis Marana, if anything has happened to Alma Crawford. (*Savagely.*) Curse you ! If she is harmed in any way, like the American Indian, I will burn you at the stake !

[JAMES *utters a sigh, struggles for a moment, and then sits up and looks around in surprise, and then rubs his eyes in amazement as he catches sight of* ROBERT *chained to the wall.*

James (*in wonder*). What, you Robert? Do my eyes deceive me?

Robert (*laughing*). No, it's I all right! But how came you here!

James. And I might ask of you the same question. When I left the camp with the Cuban spy, he accompanied me a short way and then left me. When a short distance from the plantation we met a Cuban woman with a jug of clear, cool looking water. She wanted to know if I didn't wish a drink. The day was warm and the water cool and inviting. I drank first—and that is all I remember. I now wake from my stupor to find myself chained to the floor like a dog. How I came here and who brought me is more than I can tell. (*Wildly.*) And God only knows where my dear child is at the present moment!

Robert. At all events it seems you were captured by the same means as I was, namely, drugged water.

James (*in surprise*). But I left you in camp among your own friends, and now I find you here a prisoner as well as myself.

Robert. But you see they got me just the same.

James (*thoughtfully*). And what is to be the outcome of all this, Robert?

Robert. Well, that is hard to say, Mr. Crawford. It all depends now on General Shafter and his men. Still, if the worst comes to the worst, we have powerful friends close at hand who will help us.

James. You speak hopefully, Robert!

Robert. And why shouldn't I? Sam and Pedro, the Cuban spy, are close at hand, and will help us or lose their lives in the attempt.

James. Then at least let us be thankful for that much. But have you tried to get rid of your chains?

Robert. Yes, long ago. I might just as well command the heavens to fall, as to try and break these links of iron. (*Listening; then quickly.*) But hush! someone is coming!

RAMON enters *from* R.

Ramon (*looking at the two of them and laughing*). And so it seems that two of the boastful American dogs will soon be out of the way.

Robert (*sternly*). What do you mean, you Spanish hound?

Ramon (*aside*). You shall pay dearly for that, young man! (*Aloud.*) I mean that unless the American senorita promises to marry my son, I will have the two of you put to death!

Robert (*aside*). I'll pretend I haven't heard anything and see what he'll have to say. (*Aloud.*) Who the devil is your son? I never knew you had one while you worked on the plantation.

James (*aside*). I wonder what game is Robert up to.

Ramon (*laughing*). You, like all the rest believed me to be a Cuban and in sympathy with the insurgents. Such was not the case. (*Proudly.*) I am a Spanish nobleman and came to Cuba for a purpose. You, James Crawford, should know me well.

James (*scornfully*). I am ashamed to say I saw too much of you while you worked for me.

Ramon. I mean before that. Let your memory carry you back to twenty years ago, and the city of New York.

James (*quietly*). Well, what about it?

Ramon. You can't have possibly forgotten Ramon Marana.

James (*sternly*). You mean the Spaniard who tried to come between me and the girl I made my wife?

Ramon (*sneering*). I see you haven't forgotten.

James (*laughing*). How could I forget when I had the happiness of giving him a first class thrashing. Oh, yes, I remember all right.

Ramon (*savagely*). And dearly you shall pay for every blow, James Crawford, before I get through with you!

James. What do you mean, you devil?

Ramon (*coldly*). I mean that I am Ramon Marana, and my son is Captain Louis Marana, of the Spanish army! And I am happy to say, my son is the future husband of the American senorita!

Robert (*furiously*). Curse you! If I was free of these chains, I would tear you limb from limb! (*Wildly.*) Oh, heavens! For the strength to break the accursed chains.

[*He struggles to free himself.*

Ramon (*laughing*). Have no fear, my brave American hero, they are quite strong enough to hold you and a good many more of your countrymen!

Robert. Take care they are not the means of your death in the end.

Ramon (*laughing*). I'll take chances, señor. I am going to have my son bring the American senorita into this room. I have sent for a priest who will be here in a short time and will make them man and wife, and in this very room. You, my American prisoners, shall act as the witnesses. And then the vast Crawford plantation will fall into the hands of my son.

James. You scoundrel!

Ramon (*coolly*). Remember, a Spaniard never forgets.

Robert. Nor an American either!

Ramon (*mockingly*). For the present, señors, *adios!*

[**Exit** R. *with a smile on his face.*

James. Oh, go to the devil !

Robert (*tugging at his chains*). Oh God ! will that infernal devil be allowed to triumph in his evil designs ? Oh, why don't Sam come to our help before it's too late ?

James. Perhaps help may be closer at hand than we are aware of. (*Listen.*) Hush ! I am afraid the devil is coming back !

PEDRO **enters** *from* C.

Pedro (*in a whisper as he motions for them to remain quiet*). Hush ! Señors, don't speak above a whisper, or you will ruin all.

Robert (*in amazement*). You, Pedro !

Pedro (*nodding*). Si, señor, it's me all right. I come to liberate you both. The American soldiers are advancing in this direction and may be here in a short time. The guns on the big American ships are going to commence shelling the city again. (*He produces a key and unlocks the chains of* JAMES *and then crosses to* ROBERT *and does the same for him.*) Don't try to leave this room until the American soldiers arrive, as you would be shot before you reach your friends by the Spanish marksmen. (*He hands each of them a revolver as he speaks.*) And now, señors, *adios*. [*Exit* C. *quickly.*

James (*quickly*). By George, Robert, I just thought of an idea. (*He rises and stretches himself as he speaks, and* ROBERT *does likewise.*) Didn't Ramon say he'd be back here in a short time with his son, my daughter and a priest ?

Robert (*nodding*). I believe so, Mr. Crawford.

James. Why not pretend to be still in chains, and see how far this Spanish devil will go. And then at the last moment, when he thinks he is about to triumph, step in and break up his little game ? In the meantime it may give Shafter and his men a chance to reach this building. (*The sound of cannon is heard outside.*) Hark ! The bombardment has begun !

Robert (*quickly*). It's a good idea and we'll carry it out. And when I get through with the son he will never forget this American, I reckon.

[*Both resume their position as before ;* JAMES *on the floor; and* ROBERT *against the wall.*

RAMON **enters** *from* R., *followed by* LOUIS, *who helps* ALMA *into the room ; she is very pale and faint.*

Ramon (*sneering*). So you see the whole of us are here this time, all except the priest. He will be here directly to perform the marriage ceremony ! [*Cannon heard outside.*

Alma (*struggling with* LOUIS *who holds her by the arm, and speaking faintly*). Oh, you cowards ! You shall pay dearly for this outrage ! You shall see before long what American heroes can do !

Louis (*laughing*). Very good, very good indeed ! But all this display won't do you any good. My wife I have sworn you must and shall be in spite of all !

Ramon. Good for you, my son ! [*Cannon heard outside.*

Louis. Perhaps you think this fine American hero of yours will help you, eh ? (*Laughing.*) I will show you ! (*He releases* ALMA *who crosses and kneels by her father.*) Just see how I can humiliate your brave American friend !

[*He crosses to* ROBERT *and slaps him in the face ; the face of* SAM *appears at window pointing gun at* LOUIS. ROBERT *strikes* LOUIS *with his fist ; he reels against his father and falls just as* SAM *fires.* RAMON *receives the contents of the gun, staggers for a moment and then falls to the ground, clutching his breast.* ALMA *crosses to* ROBERT, *while* JAMES *jumps up holding the revolver in his hand.*

Robert (*placing arm around* ALMA *and looking at* LOUIS). That's one blow for the stars and stripes !

[*Cannonading outside louder.*

James. And I have a good mind to give him another one !

[*Places revolver to* LOUIS'S *head.*

Alma (*appealingly*). Father, don't !

Sam (*at window waving his cap*). Hurrah ! The soldiers am coming !

[*A number of shots are heard, followed by loud cheering ; then a loud explosion and a portion of the flat falls away, through which* PEDRO *enters waving an American flag and followed by* DENNIS *and a number of American soldiers.*

Pedro (*waving flag*). At last Santiago has fallen !

[*All cheer and wave their hats.* ALMA *and* ROBERT C. ; JAMES *guarding* LOUIS ; RAMON *lying on the floor motionless ;* SAM *at window. Music.*

SLOW CURTAIN.

ACT IV.

Scene.—*Same as Act I.　Music—" Union Forever."*

JAMES *is seated at desk* R., *looking over some papers as the curtain rises.*

James. It will be a tough job to build up the plantation again, but I suppose it will have to be done. That war has cost the United States a large sum of money, and I am afraid it will cost a great deal more before we get through trying to civilize the Cuban insurgents. It seems all they are capable of is eating and sleeping. And as for work—that is simply out of the question. As long as Uncle Sam is willing to feed them, they don't seem to care what happens. All my old hands have left me, and heaven only knows where I can get any to help me work the plantation. Lucky thing for me I have still Robert, Dennis, Sam and that Cuban spy, Pedro, to help me along in the work of building up the plantation again. If all the insurgents were as brave and as faithful as Pedro, the Cubans would never have needed the help of Uncle Sam to break away from the claws of Spain.

PEDRO **enters** *from* L.

Pedro (*looking around*). Señor, can I speak to you for a moment?

James (*in surprise as he looks around*). Why, certainly! (*Quickly.*) But I hope you are not going to leave me as all the rest of my men have done, now that Cuba is under the protection of the stars and stripes.

Pedro (*shaking his head slowly*). No, señor, I am not going to leave you.

James. Well, then, what is it you wish, Pedro?

Pedro (*looking around cautiously and fingering his hat nervously which he holds in his hands*). Señor, a man has just applied for work on the plantation. He is dressed and looks like a Cuban, and yet there is something remarkably familiar about him. And yet, señor, I swear I never saw him before in all my life!

James. I am afraid your fears are groundless, Pedro. I have not an enemy in the world that I am aware of. Ramon Marana is dead, killed by a bullet from the gun of Sam Jackson, the day Santiago was stormed and fell into the hands of the Americans!

Pedro. Very true, señor. But remember this Ramon Marana had a son, every bit as bad as himself.

James (*quickly*). By George, Pedro, you are right. I had quite forgotten about the son.

Pedro. He was not among the officers of Santiago that surrendered when you allowed him to go, nor was his body found among the slain.

James (*thoughtfully*). Yes, it was rather strange the way he disappeared and left no trace behind. (*Laughing.*) And so you think this strange Cuban is Don Louis in disguise?

Pedro (*shrugging his shoulders*). Quien sabe, señor?

James. Have no fear, Pedro. We are all safe. Louis Marana would never dare to molest us now. Uncle Sam and not Spain is ruling Cuba at the present time.

Pedro. Remember, señor, Don Louis Marana is a Spaniard, and all Spaniards are treacherous.

James (*laughing*). You don't seem to have much faith in Spanish honesty, it seems.

Pedro. Can you blame me, señor?

James. Well, hardly. But, Pedro, hunt up this strange Cuban and send him here at once. I'll have a talk with him, and see if you have any grounds for your suspicions.

Pedro (*nodding*). Si, señor.   [Exit L.

James (*thoughtfully*). What if Pedro should be right in his suspicions? What if this strange Cuban should be Don Louis Marana, in the disguise of one of his men. Some of these Cubans are shrewder than they are given credit for, and Pedro is one of them. Perhaps he has sized up this stranger correctly after all. I think the best thing I can do is to keep my eyes open and not be caught napping.

PEDRO enters *from* L. *followed by* LOUIS.

Pedro. Here is the one I was speaking to you about, señor.

James (*nodding*). Very well, Pedro, you may leave us for the present.

Pedro (*bowing*). Si, señor.

            [Exit L. *after casting a suspicious glance at* LOUIS.

James. Well, my man, Pedro tells me you wish to work on the plantation?

Louis (*humbly, as he nervously fingers his hat*). Si, señor. (*Aside.*) I am safe; he doesn't know me in this disguise.

James. And why do you wish to work? As a general rule the insurgents show no desire for manual labor while Uncle Sam is willing to feed them.

Louis (*aside*). Curse Uncle Sam, and the whole American nation! (*Aloud.*) I am not one of that kind, señor. I do not wish to eat the bread of charity. And in order to live and eat one must work.

James (*nodding*). There is sound sense in all that. All right. Have you been fighting with the Cuban patriots for the liberty and freedom of the island?

Louis (*bowing*). Si, señor.

James. It seems to me I have seen you before somewhere.

Louis (*shrugging his shoulders*). No doubt, señor. (*Aside.*) Can he suspect me?

James. What is your name?

Louis. Miguel, señor.

James. Are you a full-blooded Cuban?

Louis. Si, señor.

James. Well, Miguel, you can, go and hunt up Pedro, and tell him I have engaged you for the plantation. ·He will show you what you are required to do.

Louis (*gratefully*). Oh, thank you, señor.   [**Exit** L.

James (*looking after him*). Pedro was right after all. There is something remarkably familiar looking about that fellow, and yet I can't just tell what it is. (*Rising.*) Well, for the sake of America and the downfall of Spain I am going to keep my eye on this strange Cuban.   [**Exit** C.

LOUIS enters from L.

Louis (*looking around cautiously as he enters and then draws a sigh of relief when he finds the room empty*). At last I am under this roof once more. I thought once Pedro had penetrated my disguise, but my fears were groundless. And once again I was sure of discovery when the American Crawford began to ask me so many different questions. But I passed through the ordeal in safety. Once the opportunity presents itself, and I will kidnap the girl and carry her away to Spain with me. I'll yet show these boasting Americans that they are no match for one real live Spaniard when he makes up his mind to act. Cuba may be lost to us, but we are well rid of an island full of niggers. The Americans are well used to handling them; so let them try and civilize the Cubans if they can. I am sure I wish them all the joy in the world in the undertaking.

[Exit L.

INEZ enters from C.

Inez (*looking around and sighing*). No one here. I was sure I would find Señor Rafferty in this room. How strange he seems since the war ended. How cold and distant. I did think at one time he would make me his wife, but it seems to be all a dream of the past. (*Sadly.*) Why can't I be happy like the young señorita? Is it because she is an American and I am a

Cuban ? Is not my affection as strong as hers, although my
skin is not as white.   [*Sighs.*

ALMA enters from C.

Alma (*enters just in time to hear her sigh ; looking at her
and speaking in surprise*). Why, Inez, what is the matter ?
Why are you sighing so ? Has anything happened ?

Inez (*shaking her head*). Nothing that I know of, señorita.

Alma (*quickly*). Oh, yes, there must be, Inez. Girls aren't
sighing for nothing nowadays. Come now, Inez, tell me all.
Are you not happy in this home ? (*Quickly.*) Oh, I see, Inez,
you are in love with Dennis.

Inez (*holding down her head*). The American señorita's
eyes are sharp !

Alma. Don't be sighing so, Inez. I know that Dennis
thinks all the world of you !

Inez (*bashfully*). Do you think so, señorita.

Alma. Yes, I have heard him say so, himself. (*Listens.*)
Hush ! I think I hear his voice. He is coming this way. I
will leave you with him.

Inez (*quickly trying to detain her*). Oh, señorita, don't run
away from me.

Alma (*laughing*). Don't be a little simpleton, Inez. If he
asks you to be his wife say yes, as you may lose him if you
don't.   [*Runs out* C. *laughing.*

Inez. The American señorita is indeed brave like all of
her country people.

DENNIS enters from L.

Dennis (*in surprise*). Well, may I never see heaven, but is
it yerself, Inez ? Shure, what seems to be the matther with you,
at all, at all ? Are ye sick, darlin' ?

Inez (*holding down her head*). Yes, señor, I am sick.

Dennis. Then I'll hunt up a docther, an' have him fix ye up
in no time.

Inez (*slowly*). It's something no doctor can cure, señor, but
the grave.

Dennis. What the divil do ye mane, at all, girl ?

Inez. My sickness is of the heart and not of the body, Señor
Rafferty.

Dennis (*quickly*). Oh, faith, that's easily cured. Darlin',
now that the war is over, do you think you could learn to love
me enough to marry me ?

Inez (*slowly and sadly*). The American señor is but trying
to jest with the poor Cuban girl.

Dennis (*quickly*). Divil the jest, acushla ! Cuba was down-
trodden and so is Ireland. Cuba was set at liberty by America,

and who knows but Ireland will be free in time, an' be the help av the same country ! So let us hope in the future !

Inez. And will not the señor be ashamed of his Cuban wife ?

Dennis (*quickly*). Av coorse not.

Inez. But my skin is not as white and fair as the American señorita.

Dennis (*laughing*). Shure ye haven't none the best av me, me girl. Since I came to this island me own mother wouldn't know me now, I'm so burned with the sun. So if you will only say yis whin I ax ye I'll be the happiest man on earth.

Inez. You will, señor ?

Dennis. I will that. But, darlin', I'm waitin' patiently.

Inez (*in surprise*). You are waitin', señor ?

Dennis. Av coorse I am.

Inez. I don't understand the señor.

Dennis. I am waitin' for ye to say yis.

Inez. Oh ! (*Laughing.*) But you haven't asked me yet.

Dennis (*aside*). Well, what do ye think av that ? (*Aloud.*) An' was that all ye have been waitin' for, me angel ?

Inez (*nodding*). Yes, señor.

Dennis. Thin hear me, Inez, darlin'. I want ye to be the future Mrs. Dennis Rafferty. If ye say yis all well an' gude. If ye say no there is liable to be throuble. Now thin, darlin' av me heart, will ye marry me, an' put an end to all me fears at wance.

Inez. Yes, señor, I will be your wife.

Dennis. Do ye mane that, Inez ?

Inez. The señor knows I do from the bottom of my heart.

[SAM **enters** *from* C. *with an armful of dishes ; he stops after entering the room and smiles when he sees the two of them.*

Dennis. Thin come to me arms, so that I can give ye a kiss that would sink the "Texas."

Inez. I am ready, señor.

Dennis. Thin come a-jumpin', me angel.

[*He opens his arms and she runs into them : he hugs and kisses her with delight.*

Sam (*dropping all the dishes on the floor and clapping his hands in delight*). By golly ! I'ish, that am lubly !

Inez (*breaking away from* DENNIS). Oh, señor, some one has been watching us. [*Runs out* L.

Dennis (*crossing to where* SAM *is standing*). Nagur, if I wasn't so happy I'd break your head. But as I have won the girl av me heart I am goin' to forgive ye !

Sam. I'ish, I have a great scheme. When yo am going to be married, I'll be yo best man.

Dennis (*shaking his head*). No, nagur, ye won't. Whin I

git married my best man will be a white man an' not a nagur.
Now put that in yer pipe an' shmoke it, me fine boy !
[**Exit** L.. *with a swagger.*

Sam (*looking after him*).   Well, sakes alive, but he am cut-
'nly a wahm baby !   (*Looking down at the broken dishes.*)   At
least he might have helped me to pick up the broken dishes.
(*He kneels down and begins to pick the pieces up and place them
on his arm ; as fast as he picks them up they fall off again.
After trying for several seconds, he throws all the pieces down
he has in his arms and rises in disgust.*)   Somethin' am cer'-
t'nly wrong somewhere.   I spect the best thing I can do am to
get a broom and dustpan.   I'll surely catch it from missey if
she see dis room now.   So I thinks I'd best hurry and 'scape all
kinds of trouble.   So here goes fo' the broom and the dustpan.
Mighty mean I'ishman that wouldn't stop an' help me.   But
hum !   He am in love an' powerfully bad at that.   Hum !
I'ishman am no good anyhow. [**Exit** L.

ALMA **enters** *from* C.

Alma (*seeing the broken dishes on the floor*).   Mercy on me !
What is the meaning of this, I wonder ?   Sam must have been
dreaming, to break all the dishes.

LOUIS **enters** *from* L.

Louis.   Can I speak with the señorita, for a moment ?
Alma (*nodding*).   Yes.   (*Pointing to dishes on the floor.*)
First pick up the broken crockery from the floor.
Louis (*proudly*).   Señorita, I am no servant !
Alma (*sternly*).   Then what are you doing in this room ?
(*He removes his disguise and smiles.*)   Ah, heavens, I see it
all now !   You are no Cuban, but Don Louis Marana in disguise.
Louis (*laughing*).   Correct, fair lady.   Your eyes are a good
deal sharper than the others and would have found me out
sooner or later.
Alma.   And what do you want in this house, Don Louis ?
Louis.   I came after the fair señorita.
Alma.   And do you think I will go with you ?
Louis.   You can't help yourself, fair lady.
Alma.   I will scream for help.
Louis.   What good will that do you.   I took the American
captain from among his friends, and escaped.   And I intend to
do the same with you.   So prepare to accompany me at once.
The Americans have wrested Cuba from us, and I am stealing
you from them.   It's a fair exchange and no robbery !
[*She turns to run past him when he catches hold of her
and both struggle desperately.*

Alma (*calling*). Help ! help ! father ! Robert !

[ROBERT *runs in from* C.

Robert (*quickly*). What is the meaning of this ?

Alma (*wildly*). Oh, Robert, save me !

Robert (*sternly*). Release that girl, you devil !

Louis. Yes, I'll release her, and rid myself of you at the same time.

[*He releases* ALMA *and draws a knife and rushes at*
ROBERT.

Robert (*jumping back*). So that is your game, is it ? (*He draws a revolver and points it at* LOUIS.) Two can play at that game !

Louis (*throwing knife away*). The advantage is too much on your side. I am unarmed !

Robert (*throwing revolver away, which falls at door* C.). Then it shall be man to man without weapons of any kind.

Louis. Ha ! I have you now !

[*He draws another knife and rushes at* ROBERT *just as*
PEDRO **enters** *from* C., *picks up the revolver from the
floor and fires ;* LOUIS *reels for a moment, staggers
and then falls to the ground.*

Robert (*gratefully*). Pedro, you have saved my life !

[ALMA *crosses and clings to* ROBERT.

JAMES *runs in from* C.

James. What was the meaning of that shot ?

Robert (*pointing to body of* LOUIS). We have seen the last of Louis Marana forever !

[SAM *appears at door* L. *with a broom in one hand and a
dustpan in the other.*

James (*in amazement*). Dead !

Robert (*slowly*). Yes, dead !

[*Music—" The Star-Spangled Banner !"*

PEDRO, D. C.

ROBERT *and* ALMA, C. ; JAMES L.

LOUIS, R.   SAM, L.

SLOW CURTAIN.